This

Ladybird First Favourite Tale

belongs to

....

Published by Ladybird Books Ltd
A Penguin Company
Penguin Books Ltd, 80 Strand, London WC2R 0RL, UK
Penguin Books Australia Ltd, Camberwell, Victoria, Australia
Penguin Group (NZ) 67 Apollo Drive, Rosedale, North Shore 0632, New Zealand

001 – 10 9 8 7 6 5 4 3 2 1

ISBN: 978-1-40930-629-0

Printed in China

Ladybird First Favourite Tales

Goldilocks
and the
Three Bears

BASED ON A TRADITIONAL FOLK TALE
retold by Nicola Baxter ★ illustrated by Ailie Busby

Deep in the forest lived three bears.
There was BIG Father Bear,

middle-sized
Mother Bear,

and tiny little
Baby Bear.

Father Bear had a BIG voice. Mother Bear had a middle-sized voice. Baby Bear had a tiny little voice. You could only just hear it.

Hello there!

Pardon?

Pardon?

Bright and early one morning, Mother Bear was busy making breakfast.

"We'll enjoy our porridge even more if we have a little walk first," she said.

But while the bears were walking,
so was someone else. It was a
little girl called . . .

...Goldilocks.

She had golden hair, and her cheeks were rosy.
But little Goldilocks was rather nosy!

When she saw the house, with the door open wide,
that naughty little girl walked right inside!

Goldilocks was feeling peckish. There on the table she saw three bowls of porridge, so she picked up a spoon to have a taste.

The first bowl of porridge was much too hot.

The second bowl was much too lumpy!

But, "Mmmmm!" The third little bowl was just right ... and suddenly it was absolutely empty!

Feeling rather full and sleepy, Goldilocks looked for a chair.

How many do you think were standing there?

The first chair was much too hard.

The second chair was much too soft!

But the third little chair was just right—for a baby bear. Goldilocks sat down and . . .

One . . .
two . . .
three chairs.

...CRASH! She smashed the little chair.

Goldilocks felt tired and cross after such a bruising bump. She quickly hurried up the stairs and peeked into the ...

...bedroom.

There she saw a BIG bed, a middle-sized bed and a tiny little cosy bed.

The first bed was much too hard.

The second bed was much too soft!

But, "Mmmmm!" The third little bed was just right ...

...for a snooz-z-z-z-z-z-z-z-z-z-z-e.

Meanwhile on the forest track,
the three bears were coming back.

They noticed right away that things
were wrong.

"Someone's been eating my porridge!"
growled Father Bear.

"Someone's been eating my porridge!"
said Mother Bear.

"Someone's been eating my porridge," squeaked
Baby Bear, "and they've eaten it all up!"

"Someone's been sitting in my chair!"
growled Father Bear.

"Someone's been sitting in my chair!"
said Mother Bear.

"Someone's been sitting in my chair, too," sobbed Baby Bear.

He was the saddest bear of all. There was nothing left of his little chair.

Quietly on their furry paws, the bears crept slowly up the stairs.

"Someone's been sleeping in my bed!"
grunted Father Bear.

"Someone's been sleeping in my bed!"
said Mother Bear.

"Someone's been sleeping in my bed," squeaked Baby Bear ...

Boo hoo!

"... and she's still there!"

Baby Bear's tiny voice woke Goldilocks.
She opened one eye ...
and then the other ...

Then she leapt out of bed, ran out of the house, and never went back.

And what's more, after that Goldilocks never had porridge for breakfast!